W9-CLQ-958

The Vanishing Vampire

Starscape Books by David Lubar

NOVELS

Flip

Hidden Talents

Hyde and Shriek

True Talents

NATHAN ABERCROMBIE, ACCIDENTAL ZOMBIE SERIES

My Rotten Life

Dead Guy Spy

Goop Soup

The Big Stink

Enter the Zombie

STORY COLLECTIONS

Attack of the Vampire
Weenies and Other Warped
and Creepy Tales

The Battle of the Red Hot
Pepper Weenies and Other
Warped and Creepy Tales

Beware the Ninja Weenies
and Other Warped
and Creepy Tales

The Curse of the Campfire
Weenies and Other Warped
and Creepy Tales

In the Land of the Lawn
Weenies and Other Warped
and Creepy Tales

Invasion of the Road
Weenies and Other Warped
and Creepy Tales

The Vanishing Vampire

A MONSTERRIFIC TALE

DAVID LUBAR

STARSCAPE

A Tom Doherty Associates Book
New York

This is a work of fiction. All of the characters, organizations, and events portrayed in this novel are either products of the author's imagination or are used fictitiously.

THE VANISHING VAMPIRE

Copyright © 1997 by David Lubar

The Unwilling Witch excerpt copyright © 1997 by David Lubar

Illustrations by Marcos Calo

A Starscape Book
Published by Tom Doherty Associates, LLC
175 Fifth Avenue
New York, NY 10010

www.tor-forge.com

ISBN 978-0-7653-3077-2 (hardcover)
ISBN 978-1-4299-9306-7 (e-book)

Tor books may be purchased for educational, business, or promotional use. For information on bulk purchases, please contact Macmillan Corporate and Premium Sales Department at 1-800-221-7945 extension 5442 or write specialmarkets@macmillan.com.

First Edition: May 2013

0 9 8 7 6 5 4 3 2 1

For Joelle, because
she can see the magic

Contents

Author's Note

I've always been a fan of monsters. As a kid, I watched monster movies, read monster magazines, built monster models, and even tried my hand at monster makeup for Halloween. Basically, I was a creepy little kid. It's no surprise that, when I grew up and became a writer, I would tell monster stories. I've written a lot of them over the years. My short-story collections, such as *Attack of the Vampire Weenies and Other Warped and Creepy Tales*, are full of vampires, werewolves, ghosts, witches, giant insects, and other classic creatures. The book you hold in your hands is also about a monster. But it is different from my short stories in a wonderful way. Let me explain.

Years ago, I decided I wanted to tell a tale through the eyes of a monster. That idea excited me, but it didn't feel special enough by itself. Then I had a second idea that went perfectly with the first one. What if a kid became a monster? Even better—what if the kid had to decide whether to remain a monster, or to become human again? The result of these ideas was not one book, but six. It seems the town of Lewington attracts a monsteriffic amount of trouble. To find out more, read on.

The
Vanishing
Vampire

One

A PAIN IN THE NECK

I was on my way home from a movie when the dark thing fell on me. I'd been walking quickly, hurrying to the safety of home. Lewington isn't a dangerous place to live, but I'd just watched the late showing of *Creepers from the Crypt*. I couldn't fight the urge to rush through the empty streets. Images from the film chased me as I went, threatening to leap from my mind and become real.

Just one block back, I'd split up with my friend Norman. He headed left on Maple. I stayed on Spruce, walking past that huge oak whose roots were slowly breaking up the sidewalk by the vacant lot.

I heard nothing. I saw very little. Later, thinking

back, I remembered the eyes and the teeth. At the time, I just knew darkness was dropping toward me. And the darkness wasn't only in the night; it filled my mind and took me away.

The darkness inside me lifted as I woke, leaving me wondering why I wasn't in bed. I was somewhere hard and cold. There was dirty concrete beneath my fingers. I sat up slowly, feeling the world spin. I held very still, waiting for it to stop.

I stood. The world spun again, but with less force. I put one hand out and touched the rough bark of the tree.

The tree. Something dark? Something falling? I couldn't quite remember.

I turned toward home, unsure of what had happened. I'd passed out or fainted. No. "Guys don't faint," I mumbled to myself.

Behind, I heard the scraping slap of sneakers on the sidewalk. Someone was calling a name. Someone was calling me. I turned, moving cautiously, afraid that the world would follow my motion and start to spin again.

It was Norman. He was running toward me, one finger pushing up the glasses that were always sliding down his nose. "Splat, hey, Splat, you okay?"

They call me Splat. It's a long, stupid story. My name's Sebastian. Sebastian Claypool. That name is a short, stupid story. Before I was born, Mom and Dad were listening to a lot of music written by Johann Sebastian Bach. Dad thought Johann would be a strange name for a kid. So, *blam*, they hang Sebastian on me. Thanks, Dad.

It could have been worse. They also liked the poet Percy Bysshe Shelley.

Norman reached me and stood there, taking deep breaths like a catfish dragged onto shore. Running was not a big part of his life. The night had grown chilly, and the air turned to swirls of fog as it left Norman's nostrils. "I looked back and you were on the ground," he said. "Did you trip?"

"I don't know." I tried to remember. "Don't tell anyone, but I think I passed out."

"Wow, that's bad. It could mean all kinds of things." He pushed up his glasses again. "You should probably get a CAT scan. I wouldn't rule out a brain tumor, though of course blood sugar is generally a factor in these cases, and the glucose level by itself isn't always enough of an indicator to determine—"

"Norman." I tried to stop him. Once he got going, he was like a bus rolling down a hill. If I caught him while he was just inching along, there was hope. But after he picked up some speed and really started barreling along the Highway of Fascinating Facts, there was no way to slow him down. "Hold on. I just got a little dizzy, that's all."

"What'd you eat?" he asked.

I thought back. That part of my night was clear enough. I'd had my usual popcorn—the Tub-of-Fun size that lasts about a quarter of the way through the movie. I'd washed it down with a cherry cola. Then I'd had a pack or two of caramel chews and as many of Norman's gummy eyes as he'd let me steal. Nothing there to make a kid lose touch with the world. I told Norman the list of snacks.

He seemed to be in deep thought. I imagined him running some kind of chemical tests in his mind, looking for a reaction between the assorted snacks. This could take all night. I just wanted to get home. "Look, thanks for coming over, but I'm fine."

"Are you sure?"

I nodded. Except for the dizziness, which had almost totally faded, I felt perfectly normal. Actually, I felt pretty good. Everything was starting to look very sharp and clear. As I nodded, I noticed a slight tingling on the left side of my neck. The skin below my jaw felt numb. I rubbed the spot.

"You probably should see your doctor if it happens again."

"Yes, Mother," I kidded him. Having Norman for a friend was almost like having a third parent. I noticed that the tingling in my neck was going away.

"Okay." He started to leave, then said, "See you tomorrow?"

"Sure. Maybe they got some new comics at the

shop. We can check that out." The tingling was completely gone. Everything felt fine.

"Great," Norman said. "I'll see you then." He turned and walked back toward Maple.

"Thanks," I called after him. As he walked away, he seemed, for a moment, to stay in sharp focus. It was almost like my eyes were some kind of zoom lens. But as soon as I was aware of it, the illusion snapped away.

I headed home. Whatever had happened was weird, *really* weird. I took my hand from my neck, squinting as I walked into the glare of a streetlight.

My fingers felt like they were still sticky from the movie snacks. That was strange. I looked down at my hand. For a second, I couldn't tell what I was seeing. The light was so bright. Then I saw it.

There was blood on my fingers.

Two

BACK HOME

Blood.

Without thinking about it, I put my hand to my mouth. I froze as I realized what I was about to do. I'd almost licked my fingers, like the stain was leftover chocolate. Yuck. I shuddered at the thought, rubbed my fingers against my palm, and then rubbed my whole hand against my jacket. I touched my neck again, then looked at my fingers. Nothing.

Whatever it was—a cut or a scrape or a bug bite—it seemed to be healing quickly. Maybe I hit the tree when I fell. No big deal—it was over.

I walked along Spruce, then turned right onto Birch. Whoever built this part of town obviously had a thing for trees. All the streets had tree names. My house wasn't far from the corner—third house on the right. The porch light was on. It seemed pretty bright. I wondered if Dad had changed the bulb.

As I walked up the porch steps, my energy disappeared. I felt exhausted. I mean *really* drained. All I wanted to do was crawl into bed, get under the blankets, and sleep for a couple of hundred years. I stood still and held on to the railing, wondering if the strain of climbing the steps would make the dizziness return.

It didn't come back. I went inside. The warmth of the house felt good. I shivered, suddenly aware of how cold I'd been. For a moment, I just stood in the hallway, letting the heat sink into my body.

"Is that you, Sebastian?" my mom called from the living room.

"Yup." I walked down the hall.

"How was the movie?" she asked.

Movie? The question confused me. Then I remembered. Back before the walk, before the darkness, there'd been the movie. "Great. It was really awesome. There was this guy who had this really huge ax and he—" I stopped. She wasn't going to want to hear the details of that particular film. "Where's Dad?"

"In his shop. He just got a large order for one of his new jewelry designs, and he wanted to get started on it."

"Well, I'm pretty tired. I won't bother him if he's working. Just tell him I said good night."

"I will. See you in the morning."

"See ya." I headed toward my room. Rory, my little brother, was waiting for me at the top of the stairs. It was way past his bedtime, but we sorta had this ritual.

"Tell me 'bout the movie," he whispered.

"It was awful," I said as we moved toward his room. "It was so scary, if I told you about it, you'd break out ·in goose bumps."

We weaved our way across his floor, avoiding the toy soldiers, trucks, tanks, and jeeps that made up a large part of Rory's world. He was crazy about army gear. He even had a gas mask Dad had found at a garage sale, and a mess kit and a ton of other things. Sometimes, I'd play Martian-elephant-monster—chasing Rory around the house while I wore the gas mask.

"Tell me." He hopped into his bed.

I told him. I watered it down and made up stuff to replace the really gruesome parts. He didn't need to know about the guy running around with his head flopping in two pieces, or what happened when the wizard cast the spell on the earthworms. The thought of that still made my stomach squirm. But I told him enough about the film for him to feel that he'd been there. That was our ritual. Rory wasn't allowed to see monster movies yet. But little kids need monsters, too. So I shared the movie with him.

"Like it?" I asked when I was done.

Rory grinned like a starving man who had just been given a box of chocolate doughnuts. He held out his arms and said, "Look, no goose bumps."

"You're tougher than I thought. Now, go to sleep."

"One more story. Please."

Normally, I would have given in, but I was so sleepy, I figured I'd be lucky to make it to my room without stopping in the hall to take a nap. "I can't. I'm really tired. I'm wiped out. I'm sapped of all strength." I tucked him in, then stepped away.

"Don't close the door," he said as I left—even though he knew I wouldn't. Rory hated having his door closed at night, especially right after I told him about a movie. I was just the opposite when I was his age. I always felt safer when the door was shut.

I headed down the hall to my room.

Frankenstein's monster was waiting for me.

Six feet nine and in living color. What a great poster. He was hanging out with the mummy on his left and the werewolf to the right. It was the Lon Chaney Jr. version of the werewolf. Dracula, the Creature from the Black Lagoon, and the Thing were on the opposite wall. I loved the classics.

I hit the bed like a shovelful of dirt dropping into

a pit. I just flopped onto the mattress and passed out before the first bounce.

I don't remember my dreams that night, but I think that I dreamed.

And I changed.

Three

WHAT'S THE DIFFERENCE?

I changed during the night. It wasn't a big change. Like once, a couple of years ago, I'd chipped a tooth. It was a tiny chip—so small, you almost couldn't see it. But it felt really, really big. Suddenly, there was this huge wrongness against my tongue. After a while, I got used to it. I don't even notice it now. It just belongs there.

This new change was much harder to describe, and so strange and dim that I knew I could chase after it forever without figuring it out.

It was hard to put in words. But when I opened my eyes, the world seemed different. *Sharper* is the best way I could describe it. Things were sharper—the way they are under a microscope. And it wasn't just things I saw. All my senses had changed. I could smell breakfast. That's not too strange, except I wasn't *smelling* the scent of bacon. I was smelling the bacon itself. That one drifting aroma contained the whole history of the animal that it came from.

I could hear everything. I heard the sizzle of the bacon in the pan, but I also heard the hiss of the gas as it rushed through the pipes into the stove. I heard the flames under the pan, and even the smoke as it rose through the air and brushed against the ceiling. I heard my family. There was breakfast chatter. Mom and Dad were in the kitchen, along with Rory, and Her Royal Highness, the Princess Angelina, my brat of an older sister. They were all talking at once, but I could hear each one as if no one else were speaking.

And I was starving.

I felt nothing but hunger. I rolled out of bed and walked across the room. My window faces east, and a patch of sunlight crawls along the floor in the late morning. The bright patch seemed extremely warm to my bare feet, almost burning hot. I hurried past it and got dressed.

"Welcome to the world of the living," Dad said as I stumbled into the kitchen.

"Hey, it's Sleeping Ugly," Angelina said, looking up from the piece of toast she was buttering.

"Your Lowness," I muttered back.

Rory grinned. Mom shot me a look.

"She started it," I said.

Dad spoke. "Kids . . ." Dads have these spells they cast. One word, sometimes two or three. *Blam*, like magic, they work their charms on us helpless youngsters. *Kids* is one of the weaker spells, but it works well at the breakfast table. It doesn't have the power of *I'm warning you*, or the force of the dreaded *Okay, that's enough*, but Dad isn't one to waste his power.

I heaped my plate with bacon, eggs, and toast.

"Hungering for dead fried animals and unborn chickens?" Angelina asked.

Dad said she was going through a phase. Phase or not, I was getting pretty sick of it. "And how many poor stalks of wheat had their heads chopped off for that one slice of bread?" I asked. "Think about it. There they are, happily waving to each other in the field when, *slash*, the razor-sharp blade of the harvester comes along and slices them up. Heads go flying everywhere, making little wheat screams. Then, there's an even bigger horror."

"Dad, make him stop," Angelina whined.

But I was just warming up. This was getting good. "The poor victims are dragged off to the mill. As they shudder in horror, the huge stone wheel descends, closer and closer, crushing the last of their life from them—"

"Okay, that's *enough*."

Blam. Dad cast the spell of silence. I grinned at Angelina, who refused to look back. I was pleased to see she was staring at her toast with just a hint of disgust. Score one for the good guys.

"Crush," Rory said. "Eeeeee!" He made a tiny scream, a Rory version of the death scream of a stalk of wheat. Little brothers can be pretty cool.

Dad looked at him, but didn't say anything. I saw a smile flicker across Dad's lips. But he hid it well. I guess he knew that Rory, if encouraged, would spend the rest of the day making those sounds.

I dug in to my breakfast, cleaning my plate in an instant. The flavor of everything was fabulous. I don't remember another breakfast that tasted so wonderful. I couldn't get enough.

"Glad to see you have an appetite," Mom said, smiling.

I took another helping. I was still hungry. Something was wrong. I was stuffing my face, eating like the king of the pigs, but I didn't feel satisfied. I barely managed to hold off from taking a third serving.

As I carried my dish and silverware to the sink, I glanced at the knife that rested on my plate, not yet aware of what would happen when I picked it up.

Four

REFLECTIONS

I scraped my plate, rinsed it in the sink, and put it in the dishwasher. Mom has us trained fairly well. As I rinsed the knife, I saw my reflection. I also saw the refrigerator reflected in the knife blade. But the fridge was *behind* me. My folks listen to this old song by the Beatles called "I'm Looking Through You." Well, in the knife, I was almost looking through me. I mean, I was there, but not by much.

The knife slipped from my fingers and clattered into the sink. I snatched it up and took another look.

Everything was normal. I was there. I was solid. I was worried. I put the knife in the dishwasher. I was

tempted to take another look, but I was afraid of having the transparent version show up again.

As I was going upstairs, the phone rang. "It's for you," my mom called from the kitchen.

"I'll get it up here!" I shouted, heading toward the phone in my parents' bedroom.

It was Norman on the other end. "Want to go into town?" he asked.

"Sure. I'll meet you by your house." There was no point sitting around waiting to fade again.

I got dressed, grabbed my jacket, and headed out. The morning sun felt really hot. I took off the jacket, but that felt even worse with the sun beating down on me, so I put the jacket back on. As I walked past the house next door, Mr. Nordy's dog, Browser, came running up to the fence. I stopped to pet him.

As I reached out, Browser whined, then turned and ran around to the back of the house, his tail between his legs.

Weird.

I met Norman by his place, and we headed into town. It's not a long walk—about nine blocks. As soon as I reached him, Norman started telling me all about some new software he'd downloaded. He's big on that stuff. We both like monster movies and comics. And we both like video games. But Norman is way more into computers than I am. I think they're fun, but I don't get swallowed up by them the way he does. I could just imagine him getting sucked into his computer with nothing but his feet dangling out.

"Uh-oh," Norman said after we'd walked a couple of blocks.

I looked ahead. Down the street, on our side, I saw one of life's real monsters. It was Lud Mellon. Put him together with his brother Bud, and you'd have enough IQ for half a person. They were stupid *and* mean. Getting a Mellon angry at you was like taking something from one of those cursed Egyptian tombs. Sooner or later, one way or another, doom would fall. It was always a good idea to avoid being noticed by Lud or Bud.

We crossed the street, hoping he hadn't spotted us. Luckily, Lud seemed to have something else on his tiny piece of mind and didn't look our way.

"I hate those guys," Norman said. "Somewhere along the line, a couple of their genes took a U-turn and headed back to the Stone Age."

"Agreed." We reached the comic book shop without any other problems. This place sold comics and monster books and masks and stuff and was called the Gore and More Store. "Great," I said, seeing that the newest issue of *Swollen Rat People from Another Universe* had finally arrived.

"Look," Norman said, holding up his discovery. "It's the new *Hyper Hurricane Man*."

"I'll tell you what: I'll get *Rat People*, you get *Hurricane*, and we'll swap after we read them."

"Deal." We took our purchases up to the register and paid Lenny.

"Thanks, guys," he said as he counted the change. "The new *Hawkchild* is due out next week. Should I save a copy for you?"

"Sure," I said. We headed out.

"Where to?" Norman asked as we returned to the bright light outside the store.

"Your house?" I asked.

He shook his head. "Mom's cooking." Norman's mom was a caterer. She made fancy meals for people having parties. Most of the time, she was real friendly. But when she had a big order to fill, she didn't like having any extra kids around. So there were times we couldn't go to Norman's house. On the other hand, it also meant there was usually lots of good food when we did go there, since his mom was always trying new recipes. "How about your place?" Norman asked.

"We'll have to share our comics with Rory. That's okay with you, isn't it?"

"I don't mind. He can read mine first."

"Great."

We headed back toward my house. I couldn't keep my eyes off the cover of *Swollen Rat People*. The artwork was great. Rat Masterson and Ratatattat were locked in mortal combat with the evil supervillain Ludovico Mouse-Kara. I wasn't watching where I was walking. If I had been, I would never have stumbled right into Lud Mellon.

It was like running into the side of a cow. I looked up at his face, hoping to see something other than anger. He looked down at me as if slowly digesting the incident. Then he reached out, grabbed the comic book, pulled it from my grip, and said, "Thanks."

He walked on, leaving me standing there with my mouth open, my hands empty, and a feeling that was *way* beyond mad. I would have loved, for that instant, to have the power to become something horrible and get revenge. I imagined what it would be like to turn into a werewolf and rip off his arms. Yeah, and I'd do it without even wrinkling the comic.

"He probably can't even read," Norman said when Lud was out of earshot. "He just likes the drawings."

"Yeah, but I'll bet he moves his lips when he reads the pictures."

We laughed and tore him apart with our words as we walked to my house.

Norman let Rory read his comic first. Then he let me read it. He kept himself busy by adjusting something on my computer. I don't know what he did, but he told me it would run better now that he had optimized my hard drive.

I kept thinking about how wonderful it would be to live in a world without bullies, mean people, and human monsters. At least with Dracula and

Frankenstein's monster, you knew what you were dealing with. It was people like Lud Mellon who were the real monsters as far as I was concerned.

But by that evening, I had pretty much forgotten about it. And that night, beneath the posters of my favorite monsters, the change that had begun the night before took full hold of me. While I slept and dreamed of dark, rich earth and moonless nights, while I wandered through a mist-filled land of graves and crumbling castles, I became a monster.

Five

I RISE

And then, suddenly, I was totally awake. One instant, I was deep asleep. The next, I was sitting straight up in my bed, drowning in a billion sensations. Waves of sound crashed over me. I heard a million conversations: every voice in the house washed over me, along with a flood of voices from up and down the street. The sounds . . .

A car, half a mile away—I knew exactly how far it was—rushed down the road. Two jets passed overhead—one heading east, the other going southwest. A fly walked across the ceiling of the living room downstairs, all six of its tiny legs hitting the plaster with the boom of giant drums.

That's when the smell kicked in.

I smelled an entire world around me. People. Animals. My family. Browser. Cats, squirrels, the fly. I could smell two quarters and three pennies in the pocket of the jeans that I'd dropped on the floor last night.

I could feel more than just the sheet against my hand. I could feel the weave of the threads, and the touch of the man who ran the machine that made the sheet, and the hand of the woman who sold the sheet, and beyond and beyond.

Then I opened my eyes. And nearly screamed. I slammed my eyes shut against the flood of light. It was barely dawn, the sun just beginning to rise, but the light hit me like a thousand jagged rocks. I pulled the sheet and blankets over me, and jammed the pillow hard against my head to protect my ears from the surge and crash of sounds.

And slowly, in a world where time suddenly had no meaning, I started to hold back the sensations, filter them, and sort through the waves. It was like focusing a magnifying glass. But I was juggling five overloaded senses and kept losing my hold on one or another. When I lost control of one, they would all slip and crash back into me.

Loud noises came from nearby. Roaring sounds. Words. Mom's voice. "Hey, sleepyhead." The sound was loud and slow and forceful, each word striking like a slap in the face. "Are you going to stay in bed all day?"

When I spoke, the words exploded through my head with the force of a hurricane. "I'll be up soon."

No more now, please. Even my thoughts roared.

Her steps slammed away.

And another timeless hour passed. And I gained more control of my senses.

I was hungry.

But I was afraid to get up.

Another hour passed. I had shut off more sensations than I ever knew existed. I was in control—sort of. It was a slippery control that threatened to fly from my grasp at any moment.

I had become something other than what I was.

But I had won the first battle.

And boy, was I hungry.

I didn't know what had happened. I was still too busy fighting the waves, holding off the sights and sounds and smells.

But I had made it through what had to be the worst of it.

Then, as I stepped from bed, I learned the real meaning of pain.

Six

FEEL THE BURN

I left my bed and stepped into the light of day. The light felt hot against my flesh. I could bear it, but it felt the way dripping candle wax feels—not hot enough to hurt, but hot enough to make me flinch. Then my foot landed inside the bright square of sunlight on my floor, and my body filled with the pain of an unending fire. I yanked my leg back and fell to the bed. I looked at my foot. The flesh had already started to smoke and blister, blacken and crackle.

Then it healed. As quickly as it had burned, it mended, like a movie running in reverse.

That was when I realized what I had become. My mind would not accept the truth all at once, but I knew there was no other explanation. I fought against the waves of sensations as the pain of the direct sunlight slowly faded.

"Are you getting up today?" Mom called from below.

"I don't feel good." I pushed the curtain closed and got back in bed. As the words left my lips, I tried to grab them and stop them from reaching Mom's ears. This was another of those magic chants. This was the spell of parental action. I had set in motion Mom-the-Nurse, one of the most powerful types of adult wizards.

She was up the stairs in an instant, thermometer in one hand, medicine in the other. "Open," she said, jabbing the thermometer toward my head.

I hesitated. Did I have fangs?

She jammed the thermometer into my mouth, then placed her hand against my forehead. "You feel chilled," she said. She hopped from the side of the bed. "It's too dark in here." She reached for the curtains.

"Ooob right!" I shouted around the thermometer.

She paused, her fingers gripping the curtain.

I pulled out the thermometer. "Too bright."

Mom smiled, but she was obviously adding this symptom to the list and running through a collection of conditions in a way Norman would have approved.

"Well, you just stay in bed today, and I'll get you some nice hot soup. We'll have you feeling better in no time."

"Thanks." I looked at the thermometer as Mom left the room. The mercury hadn't moved. My body seemed to be the same temperature as the air. I wondered again whether I had fangs. There was only one way to tell.

I crossed the floor, opened my closet door, and looked at the mirror there. Like an idiot, I stared and moved from side to side, then glanced around. It took a minute to sink in. I had no reflection. I wasn't in the mirror. Then my reflection flickered back. For a moment, it was solid; then it became transparent.

I heard Mom take a bowl from the cabinet. I switched on the lamp by my bed, flinching a bit from the sudden light, and held the thermometer near the bulb until the temperature rose to ninety-nine degrees. Then I put the thermometer back in my mouth.

Mom had a steaming bowl of soup on a tray. I never could figure out how she did stuff like that so quickly. "Here, this should pump a bit of life back in your veins." She took the thermometer, looked at it, nodded wisely, then said, "Just a bit of fever. You rest. Can I get you anything else?"

A coffin? I thought. *What about a nice castle in Transylvania? And maybe a drooling servant.* "Nothing, thanks," I said.

42

I spent the rest of the day in bed. I knew that I couldn't stay there forever. Now, *there* was a word that had taken on a whole new meaning for me. Up until now, *forever* pretty much applied only to stuff that seemed endless, like the films they showed in science class or some of Mr. Quib's lectures about the glories of ancient French poets. Suddenly, *forever* looked like it might become an important word in my life.

I needed to talk to someone. My folks would explode. Rory would be thrilled, but he was just too young to be able to actually help. Angelina was useless unless you needed help picking what shirt to wear with which pants or some other pointless part of "correct" living.

I needed to talk to Norman. Not only was he smart, but he had resources, too. He had a great library. He collected books on all kinds of things. So did Norman's parents. His father, Mr. Weed, taught at the state college and bought books the way other people bought bread. I mean, we had lots of books in our house, but the Weeds went way beyond that. They were always buying more bookcases.

I couldn't expose myself to direct sunlight. I'd have to wait for it to get dark.

I spent the rest of the day learning to keep the world from smashing me with sensations. The forces were strong, but my willpower was stronger. Each hour that passed, I gained more control, and the sensations got weaker. I was sure there was more to learn about what was happening to me, but I needed to take my time exploring the changes. I suspected there were things I could do that would probably freak me out. I wondered about bats and fog and wolves.

My folks were going out for the evening. They checked in on me first. I told them that I'd be fine. They left. Angelina was in charge, but I knew she'd never look in my room. If I turned into a puddle of purple slime and dripped from my bed, Angelina would be the last to notice.

The sun, my enemy, slipped away. I remained. I listened.

Soon enough, Rory was asleep. Angelina was downstairs, talking to a friend on the phone. It was time to visit Norman.

Seven

A FRIEND INDEED

I crept from bed and snuck downstairs, silent as a cloud brushing in front of the moon. Night. This was my new home; this was my world. It welcomed me as I slipped out the door. I reached Norman's house and stood out front on the sidewalk. His bedroom window was to the left of the front porch on the second floor. The light was on. The rest of the house was dark. I didn't want to wake his parents.

I went under his window and thought about throwing a pebble to get his attention. I stood there and looked up to where I wanted to be.

The window came closer.

It happened even though I wasn't trying to do

anything. It was so smooth that, for a moment, I thought the window was sinking toward me.

I was wrong.

I rose to the window. I hung in front of it, standing on air. Norman was sitting at his computer. I reached for the window. I raised it. I tried to step inside. But I couldn't go in.

That didn't surprise me. I was starting to learn which parts of the legends were true, and which parts were totally made up. I'd already found that the direct rays of the sun could destroy me, though I could survive indirect daylight. Now, I knew that I couldn't enter a home until I was invited.

"Norman." I tried to whisper, but it came out more like an order to look at me.

He turned toward my voice. "Splat," he said, waving at me before his mind took in the fact that I was floating outside his window.

When it sank in, all he managed to say was, "Guh . . ."

"It's okay," I said quietly. "Something's happened. I need your help. Ask me in."

"Umg . . . unnngg . . ."

"Look, I won't bite," I said, hoping this was true. "Can I come in?"

He nodded.

Apparently, that was good enough to count as an invitation, because I was able to climb into the room.

"You floated."

I nodded. "And I sort of have to stay out of bright sunlight."

"You're, you're a—" His mind was obviously ahead of his mouth.

"Vampire. Yeah. I pretty much came to that conclusion."

"You thirsty?" he asked.

I wasn't sure how to answer that question. There was a deep hunger in me, but everything was so new and there was so much else happening that the craving wasn't unbearable. "I need your books." Our school librarian was always telling us to check books before checking the Internet.

"Sure." He sat for another moment, then shook his head hard the way a dog shakes to get rid of water. After that, he went over to his shelf and pulled out three volumes. "These two are just vampires, this one has other monsters, as well as a really good section on vampires. Now, hang on—Dad's got a couple of good ones, too. And I think there was an article in an issue of *Smithsonian* last year. I'll check." He left the room.

That was Norman. Once the search was on for facts or answers, he just shut out everything else. Any other kid would already have run to the next state or tried to plunge a stake into my heart. Norman was more interested in running after information. I knew

I'd come to the right place. Norman's room was like a little science museum. Half the walls were filled with books. The rest of the space was taken up by all kinds of specimens. There were rocks, crystals, and all sorts of things in jars. He had a whole bunch of butterflies mounted on a board. They weren't too bad, but I tried not to look at his collection of ants and spiders and beetles. Those things were really kinda gross.

I've always been weird about bugs. I remember, when I was little, really hating the section in the encyclopedia with the pictures of bees. I didn't even want to touch the page.

Norman came back with two more books and a stack of magazines. "Try these, too," he said.

"Great."

"Hey, I have an idea. I'll put a query on some message boards." He pointed to his computer. "I'll post a request for information about vampires. We'll get answers from all over the world. By tomorrow, we'll know everything there is to know about vampires."

"I thought we were supposed to be careful about believing information from the Internet," I said.

"I can tell the good stuff from the bad," Norman said. "And there will be lots of good stuff. Experts are always happy to share their knowledge. Now, let's get started and check out these books."

Norman and I read through everything. Some of it was obviously not true, but some of it seemed pretty believable. As all the books said, I could rise from the ground. And I couldn't enter a house unless I was invited. But I didn't have to sleep in a coffin during the day. Not yet, at least.

"This is all very helpful," Norman said, "but we're overlooking one key thing."

"What do you mean?"

"Your condition didn't happen by itself, did it?"

"You're right. I hadn't even thought about that." Someone, or something, had done this to me. There was a vampire in town. Great.

"You need to locate him and find out whatever you can," Norman said.

"Yeah." I could probably learn everything I needed to know from the vampire who did this to me. He was out there. He sort of owed me some answers. I had to find him.

"Let's see," Norman said. "Where would a vampire live if he lived in Lewington?" He turned toward his computer. "We could scan the current postal records and compare them with older ones, looking for relevant changes or patterns that might indicate an individual of the suspected sort had moved into the area. That's a brute-force approach, though we certainly have the computational power to perform it. On the other hand, if we can access hospital records, or do a keyword search of local papers, we could perhaps find reports indicating activity of—"

"Please." I held my hand up, realizing something that had been tickling at the edge of my senses for most of the day. "We don't have to do anything. I can smell him."

I walked over to the window, then turned back. "You're a good friend, Norman."

He smiled. "So are you. Thanks for not biting me."

I crawled down the side of the house and returned to the shelter of the night. My skin tingled, but not from the coolness of the air. It was time to meet my maker.

Eight

CREATURE COMFORTS

Actually, *smelling* wasn't quite the right way to describe it. Maybe *knowing* was a better way to put it, or *sensing*. But I moved toward him without any trouble. We were connected. I passed several streets of large, expensive houses.

He wasn't there.

I passed rows of modest homes.

He wasn't there.

I followed the trail to the river, to a run-down, abandoned warehouse.

He was there.

I stopped in front of the door. It was locked. But I

didn't think the lock would be a problem. And I didn't think I needed an invitation. I only needed permission to enter the home of a regular person— the normal flesh-and-blood kind. There was nothing human on the other side of the door. I didn't need permission—I just needed to get past the lock.

How? How to get in?

I released myself from myself. Maybe there's a word for it, but I sure couldn't think of one. I just sort of let go and became fog. This was new. This was different. It was also scary. I felt that if I drifted far enough away from myself, if I spread over a wide enough area, I would stop being me. Forever.

I drifted under the door and formed into myself again.

He was sitting in a chair.

In the middle of the crumbling warehouse, with all kinds of smashed wooden crates and broken glass, he sat in a large leather chair. Tall shelves made of old, rotting wood filled up most of the floor space. They were loaded with worthless stuff—tubs of old motor oil, used engine parts, and other junk. One shelf, stretching almost to the ceiling, leaned danger-ously over the chair.

He was reading a book and holding a goblet of—I looked closely; it was too clear to be blood.

He raised his gaze from the page. He appeared to

be a little older than my dad. He was pretty much like the picture that came to mind when I heard words like *sophisticated* and *gentleman*.

He looked at me for a moment, lowered the book, then spoke. "Oh, dear," he said in a quiet voice.

"What did you do to me?" It was a stupid question. We both knew what he'd done.

"I just took a sip. A little bitty sip. Just enough to sustain me. It shouldn't have caused you any real problems." He sighed.

"Obviously, you messed up."

His eyes turned red and fierce. Suddenly, I remembered those same eyes burning in the darkness the night of the movie. He flung his hand out, and a force slammed me backwards, pinning me to the wall. "Speak properly to your elders," he said.

He relaxed his hand and I slid to the floor. "Sorry," I said, getting up. "I didn't mean to be rude or anything. But how would you feel if you were suddenly turned into one of the undead?"

He winced. "I hate that word. The proper term is currently *person of the night*. Look, this is nothing to get upset about. There are many advantages. You should feel honored."

I kept quiet, though I was dying to tell him what I thought of this great *honor*. I knew that anything I said would upset him, and I didn't feel like dealing with another blast of his anger.

"Besides, it's probably temporary."

"*What?*" Those were the last words I had expected him to say.

"It won't last. I took a sip, that's all. Think of it as a temporary condition. Use a bit of common sense. If every donor joined us, don't you suppose the world would become somewhat crowded with persons of the night?"

I felt a little better. "How do I go back to . . ." I almost said *normal*, but I realized that word might not be such a good choice. It was pretty obvious that he thought he was the normal one in the room. "How do I get back to the way I was?"

He shrugged. "It is difficult to say. The condition could simply disappear. But it affected you so quickly that I doubt you can shake it off like a bad cold." He smiled—slightly—and said, "Maybe you're just a natural. Maybe this is your destiny. You could be headed for greatness. You can certainly remain as you are, if you wish."

"I just want to be the way I was."

"Perhaps you will. There are many stories. Unfortunately, they are usually incorrect. I don't concern myself with such matters. You see, it isn't my problem—it is your problem." He raised the book again.

"But . . ." I needed to know more, but I was scared of getting him angry.

He looked over the top of the book. "The answers

are out there. Or maybe they are inside you. Find them if you can. Or don't. It is your affair. I'd suggest you leave now, before I grow weary of you."

I could see he wasn't going to tell me anything else. So I let go of myself and passed, as fog, beneath the door. Then I pulled back into the form of Sebastian. I hate to admit how easy it would be to get used to this kind of power. I'd never have to buy a movie ticket again.

I headed home, thinking about what the vampire had said, searching for a clue, any information I could use. But there wasn't much.

I got home just as my parents were pulling into the driveway.

Nine

SICK DAY

I panicked. My mom and dad were on their way *in*side, and I was still *out*side. I imagined how much trouble I'd be in if they found out that I'd left the house. I was so freaked, I almost forgot about my new "abilities."

I moved silently across the lawn to the side of the house, then rose to my window and entered my room. As I slipped back into bed, Mom peeked her head through the doorway.

"Feeling better?" she asked.

"Yeah, I think so."

"Think you'll be able to go to school tomorrow?"

Uh-oh! I hadn't even thought about tomorrow.

How in the world was I supposed to go to school? I wondered if they had night school for kids. I imagined my class huddled around a small pile of ashes in the middle of the school yard, poking them with a stick, wondering what had happened to Sebastian.

I realized Mom was waiting for an answer. "I don't know," I said, trying to sound weak.

She smiled. "We'll see how you feel in the morning. It won't hurt you to miss another day."

"Probably not." I watched her leave.

There was something I had to do before tomorrow morning. I had a couple of posters in my closet. I'd bought them two or three months ago, but hadn't gotten around to putting them up yet. I grabbed one— Lon Chaney Sr. as the original Hunchback of Notre Dame—and tacked it over the window with push-pins. I wasn't going to get fried by sunshine again.

I spent the rest of the night learning more about the limits of my senses. I lay in bed and practiced reaching out for sounds, picking one thing at a time out of all the noise that filled the air. It was like talking to someone at a party. Even when the room was full of voices, I could focus on the person I was talking to.

But there was one big distraction.

I was hungry.

There was a deep emptiness inside me. It was still bearable—but I knew that it would get stronger. And I was sure that in the end, it would gain control and force me to do something I didn't want to do. I gagged and shuddered every time I thought about it.

Despite the covered window, I could tell when the sun began to rise. The rays sprayed the side of the house like bullets. I stayed under the blankets, waiting for the day to pass. Right after she got up, Mom came in to check on me.

"Well?" she asked.

"Sick day," I said.

"I'll call the school. Maybe Norman can get your homework."

"That would be great." Homework. It was almost funny. The things that had played a huge part in my life were suddenly not important. Did a boy who could become fog really need to know the capital of Argentina or the middle names of all the presidents? What could I possibly need to know about solar energy beyond the fact that it could turn me into toast?

Rory came in and we played cards for a while. He loved to play Slapjack. I usually made a big show of moving slowly so he could win. I think he knows I'm doing that, but it still makes him happy. We must have played two dozen games before he got tired of winning and left.

Finally, I heard Norman at the door. He came up carrying a couple of books and some worksheets. "Your homework," he said with an expression that showed he'd also realized that when you're a vampire, homework isn't a top priority. "How are you doing?"

I shrugged. "I'm not sure. But I found *him*."

Norman dropped the books on my desk and pulled a chair up to the bed. "You did? What was he like? Was he wearing a cape? Did he have a coffin to sleep in?"

"No cape, no coffin. He wasn't very helpful. But he did say it didn't have to be like this forever. It might wear off. He also said there might be a way to change back."

Norman nodded. "I checked my computer before I came over. There are a ton of messages already, and more coming in. We're getting answers from all around the world. Come over tonight."

"Great. I'll be there as soon as my folks go to sleep."

"Okay. I'd better get home and start reading through the stuff that's come in already."

"Thanks." I watched him leave, then killed some time doing homework. I figured I might as well keep up with the work since I had every intention of returning to normal.

My parents stayed up late that night. Finally, when they were both asleep, I left home and went to see what Norman had learned.

As soon as I saw him, I knew something was very wrong.

Ten

NET RESULTS

Norman looked like he had been hit over the head with a large board. He was sitting at the computer, staring at the monitor. His eyes were glazed and his face was pale. "What's the matter?" I asked as I drifted into the room.

"Eight hundred thirty-seven," he said, not looking up.

"Huh?"

He turned toward me. "Eight hundred thirty-seven." He pointed to the screen. "That's how many replies I got. I just finished reading them. Every single one."

"And? . . ."

"*Garbage!*" he screamed. "Garbage, junk, nonsense! Eight hundred thirty-seven morons took the time and effort to answer my question. Eight hundred thirty-seven total idiots who didn't have a clue about what they were writing, who didn't have anything better to do than send me completely useless trash. This is unbelievable!" He stopped, took a deep breath, then said, "I am angry."

"No kidding. You mean there wasn't anything good in the whole bunch?"

He shook his head. "Do you know how many people just wanted to express their feelings about the latest vampire movies?"

Now I shook my head.

Norman looked down at a yellow pad next to his computer. "Three hundred eighty-five. And another ninety-three took the time to send me their opinions of the latest books. Thirty-four brave souls sent me copies of their vampire stories. Eighteen shared their vampire poetry with me. Gosh, I feel so honored. I never knew there were so many words that rhymed with *artery*. Most of the other messages don't fit into any category other than, perhaps, 'just plain loony.' To top it off—to make it absolutely, gloriously perfect— one *totally* lost person sent me, for some reason, a recipe for peanut butter fudge. That, at least, was useful."

As he spoke, his computer beeped. "Great," he said, "now I'm getting email. It's probably someone who wants to discuss the weather in Transylvania or maybe express his opinion on which movie version of *Dracula* had the best costume designer or background music." He turned to his screen and read the message.

"What is it?" I asked.

He shrugged. "This one is really strange."

I looked over his shoulder and read the email:

We must rid the world of the undead. I am on his trail. I will visit you. I do this in memory of Sonya. Watch for me.
Husker Teridakian

Whose trail? I wondered. I patted Norman on the shoulder. "Thanks for trying," I said. "Sorry you had to wade through all that junk."

"That's okay. It's kind of nice to see that there are people in this world who have even less of a hold on reality than I do. And I thought my life was boring. At least now I know I'm not at the absolute bottom of the pile. But don't give up. The information is out there somewhere. It's just a matter of finding it. I'll keep looking."

"Thanks."

"What are you going to do about school?"

That was a good question. I'd been thinking about it a lot. Our school was a large rectangle. The rooms

along the outside walls had windows, but a lot of the rooms were inside, with no sunlight. "Look, once I get into the building, I should be fine. You know most of my classes are in inside rooms. If I really bundle up, and use gloves and a scarf, I should be able to get there."

"It sounds dangerous."

"It might be. But if I want to be a normal kid again, I don't have much of a choice. It would be a lot better if I keep up with school until I find a cure." I thought about my new powers. "It might even be fun." I grinned at Norman.

He didn't smile back. "Be careful," he said. "You know what they say about power, don't you?"

"What?"

"Power corrupts."

"Huh?" I asked.

"Power can turn good people into bad people. Just remember that."

"I can handle it. Thanks for the help." I left him. I was planning to go right back home, but it was almost like the dark was calling me.

And I was hungry.

Part of me feared for the fate of anyone I ran into. This whole thirst-for-blood thing worried me. It was the one big unknown area. If I wasn't able to become a normal kid again, I would have to learn to deal with it. And I sure wasn't ready to face that problem.

Eleven

BACK TO SCHOOL

The next morning, I left home by the side door opposite the sun. I was wearing a jacket, gloves, and a ski cap—too much stuff for late fall—but I had no choice. In the shadow of the house, I put on a scarf, wrapping it over my whole face. Beneath the scarf, I wore sunglasses. I checked carefully, making sure there was no inch of skin exposed. My stomach churned at the thought of leaving the protection of the house. Finally, cautiously, I moved from the shadows.

There was no sudden burning pain. Still, remembering what an instant in the sun had done to my bare foot, I was nervous at first. But as I moved out

into the light and began my walk, the clothes did their job.

So far, so good. I headed toward school.

Browser was at the fence again. He whined. *Stay*, I thought.

He stood, unmoving.

Sit, I thought, speaking to him with my mind.

He sat.

This made me feel strangely uneasy. I wasn't exactly ready to rule the beasts. I continued toward school. There weren't a lot of kids on my block, so I figured I probably wouldn't run into anyone for at least the first part of my trip. Up ahead, I saw Dawn Easton leaving her house. I waited for her to get far enough ahead so she wouldn't notice me. I didn't want to have to explain the scarf and glasses. I'd been avoiding her anyhow. She'd been acting real strange recently, and I was beginning to think she had a crush on me.

I was completely aware of everything as I walked. My senses were pretty much under control, but I was scanning the world, taking in a bit at a time, just sampling little tastes all around me. There was a bird in the tree above me. I listened to its heartbeat. Then I listened to the *skritch* of insects inside the tree. I smelled the scents of passengers in passing cars. The man riding by in the station wagon had a pack of spearmint gum in his pocket. Behind me, a block away, two kids were walking to school carrying their lunch boxes. I could tell the contents. One kid had salami and cheese. The other—yuck—was carrying egg salad. Ahead, to the left, in a house across the street, someone was using a vacuum cleaner. Straight ahead, and very close, someone was standing, speaking words. I focused in on the words.

"Look at that little fuzzball."

Odd words. I recognized the voice right away. And as soon as I knew that, I also realized whom he was talking about. It was Bud Mellon, Lud's older and stupider brother. And he'd just noticed me. I'd been so busy bathing myself in all the new sensations that I'd forgotten about things that were right in front of my face.

Bud blocked my path. "Did your mommy dress you today?" he sneered. "Are you all warm and comfy?"

I started to step around him. He turned and reached out to grab my scarf. "Let's see who the scarf face is."

His fingers were about to close on the scarf. A lifetime of training had conditioned me against fighting back in a hopeless situation. No kid could possibly win against the brute strength and stupidity of a Mellon brother. But my new reflexes didn't listen to me. I lashed out, pushing him away. I only meant to push him back so I could run past and escape to the school.

I truly didn't know my own strength. At least, I didn't know it until that moment.

Bud left the ground. He must have felt like he was flying. He tumbled back, his arms spiraling in the air, his mouth open in an expression of amazement and wonder. He looked a lot like someone bouncing back after reaching the end of a bungee jump. *Sproing!* He flew all the way across the street, crashing to a stop in some garbage bags that had been set out on the curb. After he landed, he just sat there, staring.

I quickly checked around. No one had seen the Amazing Flying Mellon. There were those two kids behind me, but they were busy looking at some baseball cards and hadn't noticed anything. It was easy enough to tell—their rate of breathing hadn't changed. I made sure to pay more attention to the space right in front of me as I walked the rest of the way to school.

I slipped inside the building, rushing past the windows and into the darker corridors. *This just might work*, I thought. *I might be able to pull it off.*

I went to my locker and put away the sunglasses, coat, hat, gloves, and scarf.

"Hi, Sebastian."

I looked over. It was Dawn. "Hi."

"It's supposed to be a really nice sunny day. Want to go for a bike ride after school?" she asked.

"*No!*"

I hadn't meant to shout, but the image of pedaling along while the sun turned my face to a charcoal briquette had very little appeal.

Dawn turned and walked away. I felt bad, but I had other things to worry about. I glanced down the hall, and there was Bud Mellon. I realized I wasn't afraid of him, but I hoped he didn't recognize me and start trouble.

He walked right past me. I guess he had no idea who'd been beneath the jacket. I watched him trudge down the hall and join up with Lud. Then, I listened to their conversation.

"Some of those little kids are pretty strong," Bud said.

"Yeah," Lud said. "Some are."

"Pretty strong," Bud repeated.

"Yeah, pretty strong," Lud agreed.

"Not all of them," Bud said. "Just some of them."

"Yeah, just some."

I tuned them out.

School was very easy. I could touch a quiz and see the answer in the way the question had been written. No, that doesn't really explain it. Let me try again. When the teacher wrote a question, the answer was in the teacher's mind. So the answer was written in the question.

I did great in gym class, too. The hardest part was holding back my strength.

I thought I was past any problems. Everything was fine. Everything was just about perfect. And then I got to science class, and Miss Clevis brought out the slides and the microscopes and explained how we were going to learn about blood today.

Twelve

THIS WON'T HURT A BIT

"Settle down, class," Miss Clevis said. "We're going to be taking a look at human blood. We'll be working in pairs. Pick a slide and find a partner."

The room was filled with exclamations, and not happy ones. There were cries of "Yuck," and "Icky," and other hints that nobody was thrilled with the idea.

"Whose blood?" someone asked.

"Not yours," Miss Clevis said. She smiled. "Nobody has to worry. No pins, no pain. These are prepared slides. All the bleeding's been done for you."

That was a relief. I had no idea what my own blood looked like now. Maybe, under the microscope, my blood cells would show up as tiny bats or little coffins. I was pretty sure my blood wouldn't pass for anything Miss Clevis would accept as normal.

Before I could go up to the front, Dawn plunked into the seat next to me. "Hi, partner," she said, dropping the slide on the table as she set down the microscope. "I got all the stuff."

The slide hit the table too hard and made a tinkling sound.

"Oh no," Dawn said. "I broke it." She reached for the broken pieces of glass.

"Careful," I said.

She started to pick them up, then jerked her hand back. "Ouch."

My eyes followed her fingertip. I saw a small scratch on it. For an instant, nothing happened. Then a tiny red fleck appeared at the center of the scratch. It swelled upward, expanding, blooming, growing into a perfect crimson drop. A deep, dark, delicious hemisphere of wonderful . . . I shook myself. I had to get away.

I leaped off my seat and sped from the room. Some part of me, some newly gained cunning or some century-old survival wisdom made me hide the real reason for my flight behind a loud stream of gagging sounds. I held my hand over my mouth, pretending the total opposite of what I felt. Behind me, I heard laughter.

I ran to the boys' room. I burst inside. There were a couple of kids hanging out. I looked past them at the row of mirrors over the sinks. No good. I turned and dashed out. I ran right into Miss Clevis.

"It's okay, Sebastian," she said, giving me an understanding smile. "The first time I saw blood, I fainted dead away. I just dropped to the floor like a rock. But now, I can slice up a frog without giving it a second thought. *Swish, swish, snick*," she said, swinging an imaginary scalpel. "You can get used to anything. Really."

"I guess so."

"I'll let you decide. Come back if you think you can handle it, or just spend the period in the media center. Look up blood in the encyclopedia and read about what we're doing."

"That sounds good. Thanks."

I walked toward the media center, trying to regain control of my instincts.

I was hungry.

Maybe it was a good idea to read about blood. Maybe I was going in the wrong direction, reading about vampires. Those books held stories that were mostly myth, superstition, and misinformation. I needed facts.

And I needed them soon.

I was hungry.

Thirteen

TRAPPED

I read everything I could find about blood. Since I didn't know which information would be important, I couldn't afford to skip anything. Even so, it didn't take long. If I wanted, I could read the normal way. But I could also just look at a page and know everything on it immediately.

Norman found me in the library. "I got a call last night from that Teridakian guy," he whispered, looking around to make sure nobody was close enough to hear us.

"The vampire hunter?" I whispered back. The phrase left a bitter feeling on my tongue.

He nodded. "The guy wants to talk to me. He

asked me to meet him in town tonight, in front of the courthouse. I think I'd better go and find out what he wants. Maybe we can learn something."

"I should come."

He shook his head. "He might know that you've changed. He might be able to look at you and tell. It's too dangerous."

"Yeah," I agreed. "I can't let him see me. I'll hide and listen."

I got through the rest of the school day without any more problems. A couple of kids made some stupid comments about what had happened in science. I ignored them. I would have done the same thing if it had been someone else running out of the room and gagging from the sight of a drop of blood.

I wrapped up in my coat and scarf again before leaving the school. When I got home, I stopped in the hall and removed all the extra clothing. Mom was in the kitchen, with a bunch of bags of groceries. I could see she was in the middle of unloading the car. "How was school?" she asked.

"Fine. What's up?" I pointed to the bags.

"I signed up to help with the PTA dinner. The theme this year is Festival in Italy." She sighed. "I'll be baking all afternoon. Would you like to help?"

"No thanks. Want me to get any bags from the car?" As I asked, I realized that I couldn't go out without my scarf and stuff. Through the window, I could see the car in the driveway, sitting in a puddle of sunshine.

"Thanks, but there's just one more bag to bring in. I can handle it."

"Is Dad in his workshop?"

She nodded. "He's working on that big order. He'd probably like some company."

I went downstairs. There was something comforting about moving below the ground. Dad has a workshop in the basement. He's a silversmith. He makes jewelry and all kinds of other things. It was a good thing I hadn't been turned into a werewolf. Imagine what that would be like, living over all kinds of silver. If the legends were right, that was the one thing that could kill a werewolf.

"How's it going?" I called as I got to the bottom step. I had to raise my voice so he could hear me over the music. Dad always listens to music while he works.

"Great. I got a big order from the Hemnetz Company for some custom jewelry. It's a real good project. Actually, it was my idea. Everyone likes birthstones, right?"

"Right," I said, reaching the doorway. Dad's workshop was just around the wall on the other side of the stairs.

"So, I said to myself, what's something different we can do with birthstones? People get tired of the same old rings and bracelets. So guess what I came up with?"

"What?" I asked, walking through the opening into the workshop.

He smiled and held up his handiwork. "Crosses," he said, waving one in my face. "Crosses with a small birthstone in the center. Isn't that a great idea for a necklace?"

They were everywhere. All over the room, silver crosses dangled—each with a tiny gemstone in the center. A force like a giant windstorm almost threw me back. I turned my head, moving away, stumbling toward the stairs, feeling as weak as a baby.

"Sebastian?" Dad called. "Are you okay?"

"Yeah, fine. I just remembered I have a ton of home-work. That's real great about the order, Dad. Nice work. They look super." I crawled up the steps.

As I reached the top of the stairs, another force hit me, surging through my body like a jolt of electricity. I was faced with a horrible odor. It formed a wall that I couldn't pass through.

I scurried down a few steps. Above, I heard voices.

"Wow, it smells wonderful in here," Angelina said.

"It's for the PTA," Mom told her.

"How much do you have to make?" Angelina asked.

"Twenty loaves," Mom said.

Loaves? Then it sank in. She was making garlic bread. She was making a ton and a half of garlic bread. *Blam.* I couldn't go through the kitchen.

And I couldn't go down the steps past a room full of crosses.

I looked up. There was a vent above me. Maybe I could pass through there and reach my room. I tried to become fog.

Nothing happened.

Did my powers work only at night? What about my strength? I held the banister and lifted my weight with one hand. The cross and the garlic had weakened me, but my strength was still a bit greater than normal. Could I float?

I tried. Wasn't gonna happen.

So, I was stronger, and my senses were a lot more powerful. But those were just human abilities that had gotten better—nothing new. The fog and the rising were different. I guess they were powers of the night.

As I stood there wondering what to do, Mom opened the door and looked down. "Oh, there you are. I'm making extra. How about a nice, hot slice of garlic bread?"

Fourteen

THE VAMPIRE KILLER

"No thanks," I said, backing farther down the stairs. The scent was following me, sickening me, ripping at me like sunbaked, rotting garbage. "I'm going to hang out with Dad for a bit." I moved to the bottom of the stairs.

"Okay, but let me know if you change your mind. There's plenty." She smiled as she closed the door.

I was trapped. I thought about my choices. There was no other exit from the basement. Even if there was, I couldn't get past the crosses. So I couldn't go down. I wondered if I could force myself through the wall of garlic odor and run through the kitchen. But what if Mom stopped me? How would I explain why I was gagging and rolling on the floor?

What if I held my breath? No, she could still stop me. That's when I got the idea. But I needed Rory. If he came by, I could get out. But there was no need to wait for him. I remembered Browser. I had made him do what I wanted. Were people any different from animals? I didn't think I could control a stranger, but Rory and I were family. I started to reach out for my brother.

I couldn't. I had the power, but I couldn't use it. It wasn't right. To make someone from my family do something without him knowing I was the cause— well, it was just wrong. I'd have to wait for him and hope he showed up soon.

Down in the shop, I could hear Dad happily working away. The clang of steel hitting silver rose above the music. At least it wasn't Friday. On Friday, Dad usually listened to opera. That, combined with the crosses and the garlic, would have been too much for anyone, even a vampire, to deal with. Over my head, I could hear Mom filling the kitchen with loaves of garlic bread. The PTA folks would pig out tonight.

Finally, the door opened.

"Whatcha doing?" Rory asked when he saw me at the bottom of the steps.

"Waiting for you," I told him. "Can you do something for me?"

"Sure."

I told him what I needed.

"Okay." He ran off. It was that easy. He came back right away with the gas mask from his room.

I put it on, then lifted it from my face for a moment so I could speak clearly. "Now, I'm the Martian-elephant-monster and I'm going to get you."

He squealed in delight and ran up the stairs. I followed, slowly and weakly, making roaring elephant-monster sounds, walking with my arms out in the traditional monster lurch. Rory dashed ahead of me through the kitchen. I went after him.

Mom looked over, shook her head and laughed, then said, "Oh, you boys."

Angelina shook her head and said, "They're such children."

I chased Rory around long enough to make him happy and exhausted. Then I went up to my room. My parents were going to the PTA supper, and they'd told us we'd be on our own for dinner. Mom had left a casserole in the oven.

I told Angelina I was eating at Norman's, then slipped out as soon as it got dark. I headed to town. There were some trees near the courthouse. I made sure no one was looking, then rose up and found a comfortable branch.

As I was getting settled, Norman came up the street

and went over to the courthouse steps. A few minutes later, a man approached him. He was a little guy, not much taller than Norman, wearing a long, dark coat and carrying a small suitcase. I listened.

"Teridakian," the man said, holding his hand out to Norman. "From Bratislava."

"Uh, Weed from Lewington." Norman shook his hand.

"I, too, use the computer. Modern times call for modern methods. I saw your question. I knew. He is here." The man spoke with a thick accent.

"Who is here?"

"My old enemy. The undead one. Vladivost. That is his true name. He has used many others. I am pledged to destroy him. He took my Sonya." The man paused and sobbed. He reached inside his pocket and pulled something out. "Here is her picture."

I wondered who Sonya was. His wife? His daughter? Whoever she might have been, it was terrible that he had lost her, and especially terrible that he had lost her to a vampire. I didn't want to become the sort of monster who destroyed families.

Norman looked down at the picture, then back up at the man. He didn't say anything.

"She was beautiful. Yes?" Teridakian said sadly.

Norman finally spoke. He pointed at the picture. "That's a basset hound."

Teridakian nodded. "She was a good dog, a fine companion. She was my life."

Norman backed up a step. "Listen, it was very nice meeting you, but it's getting late."

Teridakian lurched forward and grabbed Norman by the sleeve. "No! Listen! He is here. He must be stopped. Look, I have everything." He fumbled open the suitcase with his other hand and held up sharpened wooden stakes. "Everything," he said again.

The sight of the stakes sent a strange feeling through my chest. It was like the way I felt when I saw the doctor holding a long, sharp needle.

Norman pulled his arm free and backed up another step. Teridakian looked away from him. "So many years," he said. "I've come so close. Many times, he was within my grasp. I know he is here. This time, I will not fail."

Then he looked right at me. He couldn't possibly have seen me in the tree, but he looked right in my direction.

Norman sprinted away.

"Wait!" Teridakian screamed. "You can help. Wait!"

But Norman was out of there.

Teridakian stuffed the stake back into the case, looked around, then said quietly, "I will find you."

I watched him leave. Then I dropped down from

the tree. This man was one more complication in a situation that was already pretty intense.

I headed toward the warehouse. It was time to talk with the vampire again.

Fifteen

A PLEASANT CHAT

It was the same as before. He was in the chair, reading a book and sipping from a glass. Even at a distance, I had no trouble making out the title. It was *A Study in Scarlet* by Arthur Conan Doyle.

He looked over the top of the book and said, "Oh, you again."

"Me again. Can I at least get some answers from you?"

He just stared at me.

"I have some information to exchange. There's a threat you don't know about." I wondered how much he would tell me in exchange for what I knew.

"Teridakian?" he asked.

So much for my bargaining power. "You know he's here?"

"Don't you?"

That's when I realized he was right. I could sense, if I wanted, where anyone I knew was at any time. It wasn't automatic. I had to search out the sensations. But they were there for me. Surely Vladivost would keep track of his ancient enemy.

"But if you know where he is, why don't you—?" I left it hanging, wanting to get him into a conversation. The more he talked, the more chance I had of learning something useful.

"Eradicate him? Remove him? Drain his body of life? Suck the vitality from his pathetic human form? Is that what you are asking?"

I nodded.

"He amuses me. And he is not a threat. At least, not to me. He could harm you if he set his mind to it. Do not make the mistake of underestimating our silly little friend." He smiled. He had fangs. I probed my mouth with my tongue. My teeth seemed normal.

"They take a while to grow," he said.

Good, he was talking. "Are they sharp?" I asked.

He held up a finger, then touched it to a fang. "Oh, my, I seem to have cut myself." He wiggled the finger. I could smell the blood. It was as tempting to me as the smell of brownies baking in the oven or pizza fresh from the take-out box.

He extended his hand. "Want some?"

I was hungry. But I was afraid that if I were to do this one thing, I would be a vampire forever. I shook my head.

"Are you sure?" he asked.

I nodded.

"Oh, well—more for me." He licked the finger, then laughed. "It doesn't stop until you feed it," he said.

"What?"

"The hunger. It is like a pulse. It will come and go at first. Throb . . . throb . . . throb. But it will grow deeper. It will become all you have and all you know and all you care about until you feed it. Then it will leave you in peace for a time. That is our price. That is the toll we pay to travel through the centuries. You had the misfortune to be nearby the last time I hungered."

"I don't want this. I don't want any of it."

He shrugged. "You may have a choice. As I told you previously, it is not my affair. I am just passing through this charming little town of yours. I don't stay long in any one place. I would return to the old country if I could, but they are too wise to our ways. A few villagers disappear, and the rest start gathering sharpened stakes. A woman wakes with marks on her neck, and the hunt is on. There is no peace in the old country. Thank goodness for the New World."

He was talking now. I had to keep him going. "But Teridakian. I heard him say you killed his dog. How could you do that?"

He spread his hands and gave me an innocent look. "Have you ever gone for a glass of milk and then decided you would prefer grape juice?"

I shuddered. This was not what I wanted to become. He might act like a guy who was sophisticated and wise, but inside, he was nothing more than a dog-sucking monster. But monster or not, he was the only one who might be able to help me. "Can you tell me anything?"

"You need to find out for yourself. I see you've discovered fog. Have you become a bat yet?"

"No."

"I highly recommend it. The wolf is a wonderful form, too. And here's something you might not find in any of the stories: You can become a swarm of flies or a horde of locusts. You can become vast numbers of any insect. Now, doesn't that sound like fun?"

I shivered at the thought of being even one insect. The idea of being thousands of them was too disgusting to consider. I knew Vladivost was enjoying this. I could tell he wouldn't give me any information I could really use. He was playing with me. "You're pretty evil, aren't you?"

I expected him to laugh at me or shout at me or toss me against the wall. Instead, he rested his chin on his fist for a moment, as if thinking. Then he spoke. "No one, no man or beast or monster, sees himself as evil. I have never risen and said, 'Tonight, I will do evil.' You have much to learn, my young inquisitor. I get very bored, and I find certain things amusing that might cause you to shudder. But no, I am not evil. I can, if I so desire, even be kind. Perhaps what you need is to perform an act of sacrifice. Perhaps there is some deed you can do that is so filled with human kindness, it will help purge your body of this condition you seem so eager to remove."

He looked at me with eyes that almost glowed. "But make your choice carefully. Do not try to quickly give away a gift that is so rare. Examine your life. Is this what you were meant to be?" He picked up the book again. He read several pages, then said, "One more thing—after a certain period of time, perhaps three or four weeks, the change reaches a point where it cannot be undone. You are still on the threshold. You have a wavering reflection. You can tolerate daylight. This will pass."

I waited to see if there was more. He remained silent. The only sound was an occasional creak from the rotting shelves. I left. But at least, for the first time since I'd been bitten, I had a clue. As fog, I drifted beneath the door.

Sixteen

INTERLUDE

I stood outside the warehouse, going over his words in my mind. There was a lot to think about, and I couldn't seem to sort it all out. I needed to clear my head. I needed to spend some hours free of worry. I could become fog and just drift for a while. But that idea scared me—it would be easy to drift into nothingness. Then I thought of the bat.

How to do it?

For fog, I simply let myself go. This was different. I remembered a friend who played golf. He was always saying, *Be the ball*.

I would *be* the bat.

I thought of the bat.

As I thought, I became a bat.

It was that easy.

I took the form in midair, hovering, flapping. I kept all my heightened senses and gained others. Sound now became a form of sight. I called out, and the buildings answered me. Everything that was solid showed up by returning my call. Even the sky responded, revealing itself by its silence. I pushed my wings against the air. I flew above the buildings.

Unlike rising, flying took effort. But it was good effort. It reminded me of running that first lap around the track in gym class, running when I was full of energy, running for the pleasure of feeling the track move beneath my feet. Now, the world moved beneath my wings.

I flew away from town and toward the woods.

My mind was empty of everything except the wonder of the night around me. I was the night.

My skin was leather. My hands were claws.

I was still Sebastian, but Sebastian was a bat. Life is simple for bats.

I flew.

And I hung from a tree by my feet and thought of nothing.

And I flew.

For that time, that countless stretch of night, there were no problems. Bats have no cares, no worries.

I flew high above the trees. I swooped and soared.

But night was beginning to give way. I hurried home and went to bed.

That morning, before I left for school, Dad came up to my room, looking worried. "Sebastian, your mom and I have been talking. We're concerned about you."

"I'm fine," I told him, trying to sound normal.

"Look, there's no easy way for me to do this. I hate to ask, but all the signs are there. You're heading for some serious trouble."

Seventeen

SAME OLD ROUTINE

My stomach dropped toward my feet. How had he figured it out? Was it the crosses? The garlic? What had given me away? Had he noticed that I never went near a window during the day?

"Son," he said, putting his hand on my shoulder.

"Yes?" At least he didn't seem afraid of me.

"Are you letting other kids talk you into doing things you shouldn't?"

I was so relieved, I almost laughed. I stopped myself in time, realizing that laughter would definitely not make him feel better. This was a serious question. "Dad, I don't hang out with those kids. I stay away from them. Honest."

He looked as relieved as I felt. "You understand that I had to find out? If I didn't care, I wouldn't ask."

"Sure, Dad, no problem."

"I better go tell your mom that she can stop worrying, too." He gave my shoulder a squeeze and headed toward the door. As he reached the hall, he stopped, turned back, and asked, "So what is it, then? Are you getting goofy over some girl?"

I shrugged. That seemed to satisfy him. It was good that he cared. But what could I say? *Well, Dad, since you've asked, I'm a vampire. If you'll excuse me now, I'd like to change into a bat and fly around town, looking for a blood donor.* No, that would not make him a proud parent.

I headed out to school a short time later. Except for bundling up in the scarf, it wasn't so bad. But I knew I couldn't keep it up forever. When I got near the school, I saw something that worried me. Teridakian was standing by the front entrance, talking with Lud and Bud Mellon. Not a promising combination.

I ducked in through the side door by the cafeteria and unwrapped the scarf. Of course, I ran right into Dawn.

"Hi, Sebastian," she said, walking over to me. "How are you?"

"Fine. Uh, sorry about that blood thing. I guess I got a little queasy."

She smiled. "Oh, that's nothing. Forget about it."

She seemed to be waiting for me to say something. The silence grew awkward. I hunted for anything mindless to blurt out.

"Nice dress," I said.

"Thanks, I wanted to look good for the class picture."

"That's today?"

"Sure. Don't you remember?"

I nodded. Oh, boy. I could just see it now—the usual ridiculous assortment of poses. One kid with his eyes closed, one kid making a stupid face, one kid sneezing at the wrong time, and one kid who wasn't in the picture, because he was a vampire. The bell rang. Dawn ran off. I stood for a moment, trying to figure this one out.

When they led us into the gym for the picture, I made sure I was on the end of a row. If there was a gap in the middle, everyone would notice. If I was at the end of a row, nobody would even miss me or realize that I wasn't there.

Other than that, the day was pretty normal. I hung out by my locker for a while after school, letting everyone else leave ahead of me. I really didn't want to attract attention when I walked home wrapped up in the scarf like a woolly mummy or the invisible man.

I was beginning to have a new respect for the monsters in the movies. All of a sudden, Dracula didn't seem like such a bad guy. I paused at the exit.

Teridakian was out there again, talking to the Mellon brothers. He'd obviously been listening and asking questions, looking for any unusual incidents that could lead him to a vampire.

"Yeah," Bud was saying, "a green jacket. And a scarf. He looked like a real jerk. But he was pretty strong."

"You'd know him if you saw him again?" Teridakian asked.

"Sure."

They were looking for me. They didn't know who I was, but they knew I was out there. Teridakian, for all that he appeared to be a fool or an idiot, had a suitcase full of sharpened stakes. Who knew what else he might be carrying? I was a beginner. I wasn't even fully a vampire yet, and I certainly didn't have the powers or experience of Vladivost. Teridakian could probably hurt me.

I went out the back door of the school and took the long way home.

Eighteen

AN ACCEPTABLE STEAK

"How would you like your steak?" Mom called up the stairs.

"Rare!" I shouted down. "Very rare!" The hunger was worse than ever. I wondered if a slab of rare meat might hold my craving off awhile longer. I could almost feel my fangs growing at the thought of a red, dripping piece of beef. The scent of it pulled me down the stairs to the table.

"That's dead and bleeding," Angelina said when we were all seated and digging into our food. "How can you eat it?" She shuddered.

"Leave your brother alone," Dad said.

"He's an animal," Angelina muttered, picking at a plate of broccoli and carrots.

I ignored her. I was enjoying the steak. But I wondered whether it was human enjoyment or if it meant I was just one step closer to becoming a vampire forever. But right now, it didn't matter. I held every morsel in my mouth, slowly biting into each moist and tender piece, feeling the warm juices trickle down my throat.

If only it had lasted.

The hunger returned soon after I left the table. Rare steak, it seemed, was no answer.

I told everything to Norman later that evening at his house. "Maybe you can think of something," I said.

"It's pretty bad?" he asked.

I nodded. "Remember when you were real little? Did you ever get stuck somewhere, like in the car or on a bus, and you were thirsty or hungry and there wasn't anything for you?"

"Sure."

"Now that we're older, we can handle that. But a little kid just feels the hunger and wants it to end. That's how I am right now. I just feel the hunger."

Norman looked down at the floor for a while. Then, quietly, he said, "If you really can't stand it . . ."

I waited.

"You can have some of mine."

At first, I couldn't speak. Finally, I shook my head and said, "I can't do that."

He looked up at me. The room, without me, was reflected in his glasses. "I mean it. Maybe, if you just took a sip, you'd feel better and nothing would happen to me. And if something did, that wouldn't be so bad. We'd be in this together."

He was a better friend to me than I ever was to him. "Thanks, but it won't come to that."

He almost looked disappointed. Then he brightened. "I know, let's try to find something to take the place of blood. I mean, the steak helped you for a little while. Let's analyze the situation and try to determine the relevant factors that reduced your reaction. Then we can amplify the essential elements. Wait right here."

He ran off downstairs, leaving me alone to figure out what he had just said. Below, I heard the refrigerator open and close. Then I heard the blender. He came running back, looking real proud, carrying a glass full of thick, brown glop. "Good thing Mom just stocked up for her next catering job. Here, let's start with this."

"What is it?" I asked.

"No, no." He shook his head. "This is like a clinical study. If you know, it might skew the results. Just try it."

I took a sip. The hunger flickered. But it remained. I drank the rest.

"Well?"

"It helped for a minute. What was it?"

Norman grinned. He pulled out one of his yellow writing pads. "Liver. Actually, there were two elements in the test. One is the blood content. The other is the endothermic transformation."

I felt like I'd suddenly landed in Paris. English wasn't the main language spoken here. "The what?"

"The change brought about from the exposure to heat. The steak you had for dinner was rare, but it was cooked. That has to change the structure of the proteins. So, for starters, we remove that element." He looked like he had just discovered something important, like gravity or popcorn.

"Heat . . ." I let it sink in. And then I almost threw up. "*You fed me raw liver?*"

Norman shrugged. "Your body should be immune to any latent bacteria. Okay, that wasn't the answer. What should we try next?"

"You fed me raw liver!" I wiped my tongue with my sleeve.

"I think we need to isolate the key components. Blood is extremely complex in some senses, but nearly trivial in others. I know! Wait here."

He ran off again. The refrigerator opened and

closed again. The blender whirred. The evening wore on. Norman tried everything he could think of, which was a lot more than the average person could think of. Much to my surprise, cat food isn't all that bad, except for the little jellylike bits and the occasional crunchy part.

None of it got rid of the hunger for more than a moment. That wasn't great. But something even more disturbing happened. At one point, as he was racing into the room with a glass of blended chicken lungs, Norman stubbed his toe hard against the leg of his desk.

I watched him hopping around in pain, and it wasn't until a few minutes later that I realized what was missing. Part of *me* was missing. I was just watching, as if the whole thing were happening on a movie screen. I didn't feel any concern. I didn't feel any need to ease his pain.

I didn't feel anything human.

It was the first clear sign that I was losing the battle.

Nineteen

LOSING THE GRIP

The night welcomed me as I left Norman's house. It would be so easy to slip into darkness and leave the day world. I could see myself living as a creature of the night. I would find a place where I was safe during the day, safe and undiscovered. Then I would rise with the night.

Nearby, I heard steps. I knew them. Like Vladivost, I also had an old enemy to deal with. I ran through the night. I ran toward the steps. As I started to move, I was on two feet. By the end of the block, I had dropped into the sleek form of a wolf. I moved like an arrow through the darkness, silent, speeding toward my victim.

He was ahead of me, less than a block away now. At first, he didn't even notice what was hurtling toward him. He was just leaving the park.

"Hey, doggie," Lud said when he finally looked in my direction.

I growled.

"Nice doggie?" Lud's voice grew cautious as I rushed closer.

I leaped, hitting him in the chest, knocking him down. He rolled to his knees. I stood, growling, waiting for him to flee. He would run and I would let him run. But I'd circle him and be waiting. Wherever he ran, I would be there ahead of him. I would be his nightmare.

Run, I thought, quivering in eagerness, holding back until he made his move.

He started to cry.

I growled again and moved a step closer. He dropped to the ground, curled into a ball, and wrapped his arms around his head. His body shook as he sobbed.

Another instant, and I knew I would tear into him. Every instinct was pushing me to attack him. But one tiny human spark inside me held me back. I turned and ran through the night. I raced the streets as a wolf. My path brought me to where I'd been headed before I heard Lud's footsteps. When I saw my home, I returned to human shape.

It would be so easy to melt into the night.

The thoughts were strong. I stood outside my house, seeing a place that was all I knew and yet so different, so strange.

Finally, I went inside. It was still home for now.

"Mom and Dad are out. I'm in charge," Angelina said instead of hello.

Home sweet home.

Rory came running up to me. "Tell me a story," he demanded.

"Not now."

"Please." He tugged at me.

"Go away."

"I hate you!" he screamed as he rushed from the room. I heard him race upstairs and slam his door. He must have been really angry to shut himself in. Deep inside, faintly, a part of me felt bad. But mostly, it was just something that didn't really matter.

"Nice going," Angelina said.

I ignored her and left the room. I stopped in the bathroom and checked the mirror. If I could become a bat or a wolf, could I become a human? There was just the faintest hint of my reflection. I willed myself to become human.

Nothing changed.

For half an hour, I stood there, trying to become what I once had been. It would have been such a simple and wonderful solution, if it had worked. If anything, my ghost of a reflection grew even fainter.

I went to my room, pulled the poster from the window, and gazed out into the beautiful night.

I was less human.

And I was hungry—almost unbearably hungry. I was like that thirsty little kid, sitting in bed, needing a drink but afraid to leave the safety of the blankets for the terrors that lurked in the dark hallway.

And I knew that once I started, I could never stop. I was sure that the first drink would pull me forever from the human world.

That's how it would have to be. It was my fate.

I put my hand against the window. This would be easy. I could fly until I found what I craved. Perhaps Lud was still curled up by the park. If not him, there would be others. Someone would be out there for me. I thought of what Miss Clevis had said about blood. You can get used to anything. Yes. She was right. Anything. I raised the window, wondering whether to hunt as a bat or a wolf or a boy.

Rory's call broke my thoughts. "Sebastian! Help! I can't get out."

Even now, though I was more a monster than ever, his voice had some effect on me. I went down the hall to his room. I tried his door. It was locked. "Just unlock it," I said.

"I can't. I tried. It's stuck. Get me out." He was starting to sound scared.

I could easily break the door with my vampire

strength, but that would be hard to explain. "Look, I can get you out," I said, "but you have to promise to close your eyes. Okay?"

"Why?"

"Just promise," I said.

There was a pause. Then he said, "I promise."

"Are they closed now?"

"Yes."

"For real?"

"*Yes!*"

I became fog and moved beneath his door. Then I became me. He was standing there with his hands over his eyes. "Okay, you can look."

He dropped his hands. Then his mouth fell open. "How'd you do that?"

"Magic," I said. He'd slammed his door so hard that the latch got jammed. I fiddled with the knob until I got it working. Then I opened the door.

Angelina was waiting on the other side for me. Her face was pale and her eyes were wide, as if she'd witnessed an unimaginable sight. She must have seen me pass beneath the door. Finally, she spoke. She only said three words. But those words struck me like a stake in the heart.

"What are you?"

Twenty

KITCHEN CHEMISTRY

So I told them. It didn't much matter. I was pretty sure I would be gone soon. I told them everything. Rory thought it was a story. He just kept grinning and asking me to tell him more. I expected Angelina to run screaming from the house. I expected her to faint or start crying. I expected her to do almost anything but what she did.

"Maybe I can help," Angelina said.

It was my turn to be stunned into silence. "How?" I asked, after I had recovered from the shock of her offer.

"Those things Norman made. They were all made from meat. He was trying to duplicate blood. Maybe it would work better to replace it. The right balance of proteins, certain amino acids—maybe that's what you need. Come on." She raced to the kitchen.

I followed her.

"We could probably use him," she said. "He's a weird little nerd, but he does know a lot. Why don't you call him."

"Good idea." I called Norman and asked him to hurry over. While we waited, Angelina started pulling everything from the refrigerator and from under the counters. She soon had a pile of vegetables spilling off the table.

"I thought something was wrong with you," she said.

"Why?"

"You weren't constantly tormenting me," she said. "When you stopped teasing me, I knew it wasn't the real you."

"I'll just have to tease you twice as much later," I said, though I suspected there would be no later.

Angelina smiled and started sorting through the food.

When Norman arrived, he and Angelina immediately got into a combination argument and discussion.

"How could you concentrate on meat and totally ignore other forms of protein?" Angelina asked him. "That's such typical male thinking. Meat, meat, meat. The great hunter. Hah!"

Norman shook his head. "Look, I focus on one thing at a time. I investigate, I experiment, then I move to the next step. Who made you the expert on research methods?"

"This isn't research, it's my brother."

"Still, we have to be systematic," Norman said.

Angelina threw her hands in the air. "But you overlooked the whole role of bioflavonoids."

"Oh, my gosh!" Norman exclaimed, looking at me. "She's right!"

I didn't have the slightest clue what they were talking about. I wandered into the living room for the dictionary while they kept ranting about bio this and bio that. Behind me, I heard the blender firing into action. According to the dictionary, a bioflavonoid is something found in plants that helps build small blood vessels in the human body. I wandered back to the kitchen just in time to have a glass thrust at me.

"Drink," Angelina ordered.

"What's in it?" I asked.

"All kinds of good things," she said.

It was thick and green. But after drinking kidneys, livers, chicken lungs, and who knew what else, a bit of green glop didn't worry me. I took a sip.

"Well?" Norman asked.

I smiled. "Tastes like chicken."

"What?"

"Just kidding." I slugged it down. As the initial chill

wore off, my tongue started to burn. "Yow! What did you put in here?"

Norman and Angelina looked at each other, puzzled. From behind them, Rory giggled. He held up a bottle of Louisiana Flaming Pepper Sauce that one of Dad's friends had given him as a joke. "I helped when they weren't looking," he said.

"Other than that, how do you feel?" Norman asked.

I put the glass down and concentrated on my feelings. This was amazing. The hunger seemed to have gone away. I was free of the terrible craving. I waited cautiously, wondering if the hunger would return like it had all the other times. It seemed to stay away. "It worked," I told them.

Suddenly, everyone was jumping up and down and hugging. Everyone but me. "What's wrong?" Angelina asked when she noticed.

"It's great about the blood substitute," I told her, "but I'm still a vampire. I still need to find a way to become human again."

Twenty-one

A LITTLE GIFT

I asked them to whip up another batch of the blood substitute, without any special ingredients from Rory, and I had Angelina write down an extra copy of the formula.

"What for?" Norman asked.

"I'd like to give it to someone." I remembered what Vladivost had said about wanting to return to the old country. With the blood substitute, he could go back without attracting attention. He could go where he wished and be what he wanted. At least someone would be happy.

With the hunger under control, I was able to give my full attention to enjoying the night. The darkness was like a warm and comforting jacket.

As I reached the warehouse, I knew that something was wrong. Someone had hung garlic from the door. A window next to the door was smashed. I moved around to the back of the building, eager to put some distance between myself and that awful stench. Even the brief exposure to the garlic had made me feel weak. In the rear of the warehouse, I found a window with a large crack in it. That would do. I set down the bottle on a ledge by the window. As I became fog, I listened to voices from inside.

"At last. You will not escape me this time."

I knew the voice. It was Teridakian. I drifted through the crack, then took human form again and moved closer.

Vladivost was in his chair. His glass lay shattered on the floor by his side. The book lay next to it, slowly absorbing the spilled liquid. The vampire cringed and tried to move deeper into the chair and farther away from Teridakian.

"I have you now," Teridakian said. He held up a large cross. Even from where I stood, I could feel my strength drain. In his chair, Vladivost must have been as powerless as a baby.

Teridakian reached into the suitcase at his feet. He pulled out a wooden stake. "I've waited half a lifetime for this," he said. "My moment is here."

I thought of leaving before I was noticed. It would be easy to slip back out. But I couldn't leave Vladivost

like that. Even if he was a monster, I couldn't let this happen to him.

There had to be a way to save him. But I couldn't get near Teridakian while he held the cross.

There were rows of shelves between us. I pushed against the nearest one. It creaked.

Teridakian looked up.

I froze and held my breath. Teridakian turned his attention back to Vladivost. I pushed again. The shelf didn't give. My strength was still limited by the garlic and the cross.

"This is for all those you have harmed," Teridakian said.

I remembered what Vladivost had said about a swarm of flies—flies and other insects. The thought was enough to make me shiver.

Teridakian raised the stake.

I had to do the unthinkable. Wishing there were any other way, I left myself a thousand times. And a thousand more. And a thousand more.

I swarmed across the floor.

Even in this tiny form, I could feel the power of the cross. But there were thousands of me, and the task for each was small. I attacked the front supports of the shelf. As I worked, thousands of me watched the vampire and the vampire hunter with countless eyes. Teridakian was about to thrust the stake.

"Are you suffering?" he asked. "Do you like being a victim?"

I hurried all my selves. Thousands of termites chewed at the shelf.

It tilted.

It leaned farther forward.

It fell.

It hit the next shelf, which fell and hit the next, which fell and hit the next. Giant dominoes, they toppled toward the vampire and the vampire killer.

Teridakian looked up just as the closest shelf was falling. He dropped the stake and cross and put his hands out. The cross swung from the cord around his neck. The shelf fell onto the two enemies.

I became me again as objects crashed down and spilled across the floor. I couldn't move or think. The horror of what I had been was almost more than I could bear. Even though I was back in human form, I wanted to escape from my own flesh. I lay on the floor, feeling my muscles twitch and jerk. After a while, I managed to look up.

There was motion beneath all the shelves. Vladivost came crawling out. "Well," he said, brushing himself off and walking over, "that was certainly exciting."

"You find a close encounter with a sharp stake exciting?"

"After nine hundred years, it does take something major to hold my interest."

There was a moan from beneath the shelves. "It appears my old enemy has survived to hunt me anew," Vladivost said.

"This is a game for you, isn't it?" I asked.

"Isn't everything?"

I had no answer. I went to the back window, opened it, and got the bottle I had left outside. There was no reason to give it to him. He had done nothing for me. He was responsible for my condition. Still, I held up the bottle. "This takes away the hunger. You can go back to the old country if you want. You won't have to drink any blood. It contains—"

"Bioflavonoids, and various other vegetable ingredients," he said.

The bottle almost slipped from my fingers. "You know the formula?"

He nodded. "It works longer than anything else. Unfortunately, it doesn't last. The universe is not that generous—there is no substitute for blood. The hunger grows worse each time. This mixture can hold off the craving for a while, but it is not a substitute." He shrugged. "On the other hand, it makes a nice treat. I especially recommend it with a dash of Flaming Pepper Sauce." He smacked his lips. "Now, if you'll excuse me, I think it is time I searched for a more peaceful location."

He climbed out the window, leaving me holding a bottle that did not hold any answers.

I didn't know what to say. Vladivost's words had crushed the life from my last chance for a normal existence. I threw the bottle against the wall, and watched my false hope drip onto the floor.

Teridakian was starting to crawl from beneath the rubble. I could see he still wore the cross around his neck. Even if I wanted to help, I couldn't get close to him. I felt weak from the cross and from the garlic at the door. Everything felt a bit shaky. I was dizzy. The world was throbbing in and out of focus. It was time for me to go.

"Curse you!" Teridakian pulled himself free and stumbled toward me, the cross in one hand. He fell to his knees. Then he tried to rise. The shelves must have stunned him pretty badly. He fell again. He reached into a pocket with his other hand. "Feel the power of holy water!" he shouted as he threw something.

I turned and crawled through the window. Something splashed against my back. I felt weaker by the moment. I staggered into the night.

Twenty-two

A DECISION

I hurried away from the warehouse, still weak and dizzy. Everything had turned hazy and flat. The water Teridakian threw seemed to have drained even more of my powers. I was confused, not really sure where I was going. Eventually, I looked up and saw my house. Norman, Rory, and Angelina were waiting for me.

"It doesn't work," I told them.

"What?" Norman asked.

I explained that the vegetable drink was only a temporary aid and that, sooner or later, I would be forced to seek blood. I suspected it would be very soon. When the substitute wore off, I was pretty sure I wouldn't be able to control the thirst any longer. "Rory, could you go get my monster book?"

"Sure." He scooted off to my room.

"I didn't want him to hear this," I told them. "I have to leave. I can't go on like this. I have almost no reflection. I can't survive exposure to the sun. Worst of all, I know that sooner or later, I'll harm those I care for. I have to leave."

"Sebastian . . . ," Angelina began.

I nodded. I understood what she was trying to tell me. "It's best this way. I think I can hold on for one more day. I'll go to school and say my good-byes."

She was starting to cry. Norman looked a little wet around the eyes, too. "I have to rest," I told them. It was odd. Usually, I didn't get tired very easily.

I met Rory on the stairs and took the book from him. "Thanks."

"Read it to me?" he asked.

"Maybe tomorrow." I went to bed and slept a black, unbroken sleep until morning. This was the first night I had slept since the full force of the change took over my body.

Breakfast with my family was difficult. I think I acted normal enough to keep them from getting suspicious. I just had juice and toast. I didn't want to have to stare at my missing reflection in the silverware. Angelina, who I was seeing in a new light, also tried to act as if nothing were wrong, though she did look troubled.

After breakfast, I gathered my books, put on my jacket, scarf, and sunglasses, and left for school. If this was to be my last day among regular people, I was determined to make it a day I would remember. I would see my friends, my school, my teachers, and then come home for one last meal with my family.

After that, I would slip away in the night and find a new place to live. I imagined myself traveling the world like Vladivost. Though, of course, I wouldn't have his European charm. But I would develop charm of my own.

I didn't want to leave. I saw no way to stay.

I was so wrapped up in these thoughts as I walked that I didn't see the three of them coming.

They must have been hiding behind parked cars. They hit me hard, pushing me against a tree.

"It's him!" Bud Mellon shouted as he grabbed my right arm.

"Got him!" Lud Mellon said, forcing back my left arm.

I should have been able to fling them like bits of paper. But something had stolen my strength. I looked up.

"Stay where you are, evil one." Husker Teridakian faced me, holding up his cross. "I have found you. The light of the sun will cleanse the earth of your foul presence. The old evil one may have escaped for now, but I will atone for my failure with your destruction."

He reached out toward my scarf. I jerked my head to the side. I felt his fingers grab the cloth. I looked around desperately for some way to save myself before he exposed my flesh to the burning light of the sun.

There, on the lawn behind him, was Browser. *Attack*, I thought, sending the dog a command to leap the fence and pounce on those who wanted to harm me.

The dog didn't move.

So this was how it was to end. Here I had been tortured by the thought of spending an eternity as a vampire, and I was about to be crisped into ashes before I could begin my new existence.

I tried to yank my arms free. It was no use.

"*Die, vampire!*" Teridakian shouted, tearing the scarf from my head. The sunglasses went flying. The scarf flapped in his hands.

I shut my eyes against the sunlight and braced for agony.

"*Die, evil one!*"

Had time slowed down? Surely by now I would feel my skin turning to cinders.

"*Back to ashes, undead monster!*"

Nothing happened.

I opened one eye. Then I opened both. Sunlight fell on my face. It felt good. I blinked. I looked at Lud and Bud. I looked at Teridakian. I understood.

Teridakian didn't. He backed up, his face squishing together in a puzzled expression.

"Perhaps you made a mistake?" I suggested.

Teridakian stared at me. He took the cross and pressed it against my forehead.

I stared back. "You made a mistake. Leave me alone."

He lowered the cross. He stared at me for a moment more. Then he sighed and walked off.

"Guys," I said to Lud and Bud, "maybe you should let me go."

"Sorry." They dropped my arms and stepped back.

"He told us to do it," Bud said.

"He said you were a vampire," Lud said.

"I'm not a vampire," I said. I was me again. My decision to save Vladivost must have saved me, too. I had helped the person responsible for all my problems. Even though the thought of turning into all those termites had disgusted me, I did it because it was the only way. And I had offered him the formula. What could be more human than that? From the instant I rescued him, I had begun to change back. That was why I was so weak leaving the warehouse. That was why I had no strength against Lud and Bud, and why I had slept last night.

I wasn't a weak vampire; I was just a normal human. After having the strength of a vampire, the human form seemed so weak. But I knew I would get used to it again.

They were still standing there. I wasn't frightened. I looked at Lud. There was something I had to try to understand. "Why did you take my comic book?"

"Huh?"

"Last week. You took my comic book."

"I wanted it," he said.

"It's mine. I want it back.

He looked extremely confused. Then a slight bit of understanding showed on his face. "Oh," he said, nodding. He reached into his pocket and pulled out a folded, crumpled comic. He held it out to me.

"That's okay. Keep it."

"Really?"

"All yours," I said.

"Hey, you're okay. Thanks."

I turned from them and walked toward school. The warm sun felt wonderful on my face. I was beginning to understand something else. Like just about everything in life, the word *monster* was not a simple concept. Vladivost was right about that—no one sets out to be evil.

"Splat!"

I looked ahead, squinting. I could no longer zoom in on things, but I recognized the voice. Norman came running toward me. I'll say one thing for him—he figures stuff out pretty quickly. "You're back!"

I nodded.

"How?"

I explained what had happened. At one point, the Mellon brothers walked past us. Norman tensed, but I told him not to worry. "They won't hurt you," I said.

I finished my story. Angelina came by, and I gave her the good news that I would be able to torment her again. She seemed pleased.

Norman and I continued our trip to school. We walked into the building together. I felt great. Dawn was at her locker. I realized I hadn't been very nice to her. This was my chance to make up for things.

"Hey," I said, walking up to her, "if you're still interested in that bike ride, I wouldn't mind."

"Oh, sorry," she said, giving me a sweet smile. "I tried and tried, but you just didn't seem interested. Well, I'm going to be pretty busy from now on." She turned and walked down the hall. She strolled right up to Lud Mellon. I watched, my mouth half open, as the two of them walked off, talking and giggling. You could almost see hearts and bluebirds swirling around their heads.

"Go figure," Norman said.

"Yeah." But I guess Dawn was way ahead of me. She saw something special in Lud. Where the rest of us just saw something to fear and hate, she saw something to like.

That's how life was. One day, you're a monster. The next day you're a person. *Blam.*

Kids can be such monsters...literally!
Especially at Washington Irving Elementary. Read on for a sneak peek at
The Unwilling Witch....

I almost walked right past the woman.

She was huddled on a bench, so quiet that I didn't pay any attention to her at first. But her trembling caught my eye. She was scrunched up and shaking all over. I was on my way to meet my friend Jan at the edge of the park across from the mall. Usually, I got there first. This time, Jan would have to wait.

"Are you all right?" I moved closer, hoping I could figure out what was wrong.

She didn't answer me.

"Ma'am, are you okay? Do you need some help?"

She raised her head.

I saw a doll once with a face made from a dried apple—all deep, dark wrinkles and hard ridges. That was her, but she looked even older than that doll. Her eyes stared past me into the distance.

I tried to get her attention. "Should I go for help?" I reached out to touch her shoulder and let her know I wasn't running away. "I'm coming back. Don't worry—I'll bring someone who can help. You'll be fine."

Her right hand shot out and clutched my wrist. It was so quick and unexpected, I shrieked in surprise.

"No time," she whispered.

"There's time," I told her. "There's always time. Let me get help."

"The moment for passing is here." She searched the park with her eyes as she spoke. "It must be now. Now or never. Now or lost forever."

I tried to step back. I didn't want to hurt her, but I had to break loose. I expected to slip easily from her withered fingers, but they held me like her hand was a steel claw. "It's okay. I can get help. Just let me go. Please." I tried to stay calm, but I hated the feeling of being trapped.

Her grip tightened. She pulled me closer, then raised her left hand toward my face. "Mine is done," she said, slowly and clearly. "Yours has begun."

As she touched me, a blast of power surged through my forehead. It was like walking in front of a giant water hose. The force washed over me with so much strength that I was thrown free of her grip. I hit the ground hard. I looked up, expecting her to be tossed over the back of the bench. I winced at the thought of those old, brittle bones breaking. But she was on her feet.

"Wait." I couldn't let her move.

She faced me for a moment. "Wisdom and kindness," she said. Then she sped away. The helpless, shivering woman fled down the path, fast as a young girl, gaining speed with each step, her black dress flapping behind her in the breeze like a flock of ravens.

About the Author

David Lubar grew up in Morristown, New Jersey. His books include *Hidden Talents*, an ALA Best Book for Young Adults; *True Talents*; *Flip*, a VOYA Best Science Fiction, Fantasy, and Horror selection; the Weenies short-story collections *Beware the Ninja Weenies*, *Attack of the Vampire Weenies*, *Invasion of the Road Weenies*, *In the Land of the Lawn Weenies*, *The Curse of the Campfire Weenies*, and *The Battle of the Red Hot Pepper Weenies*; and the Nathan Abercrombie, Accidental Zombie series. He lives in Nazareth, Pennsylvania. You can visit him on the Web at www.davidlubar.com.